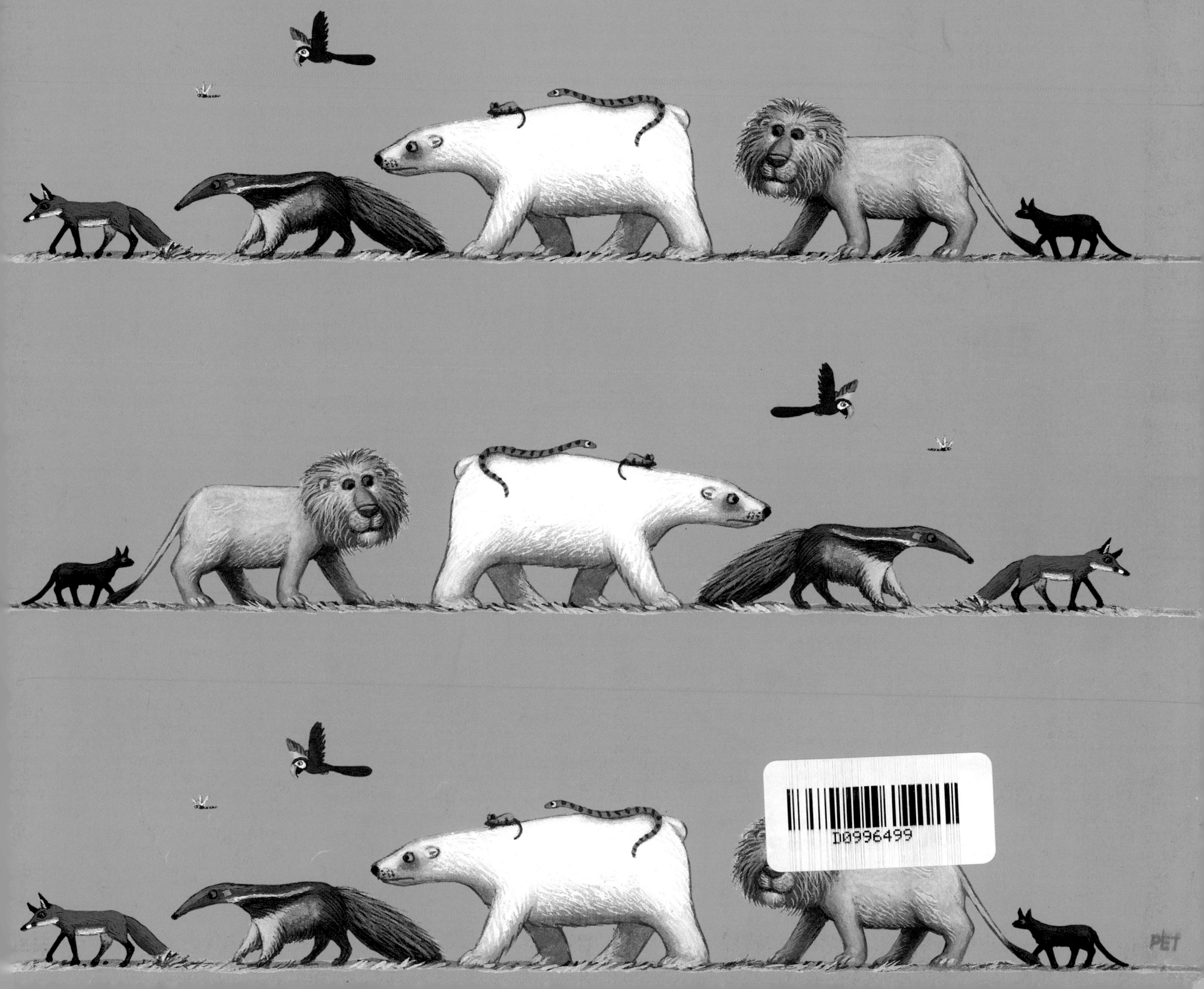
PET

To Beatriz O'Grady — BP
To my partner Lindsey — MT

First published in Great Britain in 2000 by Bloomsbury Publishing Plc
38 Soho Square, London W1V 5DF

Text copyright © Brian Patten 2000
Illustrations copyright © Michael Terry 2000
The moral right of the author and illustrator has been asserted.

A CIP catalogue record for this book is available from the British Library.
ISBN 0 7475 4659 2

Designed by Dawn Apperley

Printed and bound in Hong Kong / China by South China Printing Co.

1 3 5 7 9 10 8 6 4 2

Little Hotchpotch

Brian Patten and Michael Terry

BLOOMSBURY CHILDREN'S BOOKS

One day a shy little creature looked at its reflection in a frozen pond. All it could see were its eyes.

They were as big and as bright as the moon.

The little creature had no idea who it was, so it asked the polar bear, 'Excuse me please, can you tell me who I am?'

'You have the most wonderfully coloured feathers,' sighed the polar bear, 'they are like rainbows. But I don't know who you are. Let us go to the jungle and ask the parrot.'

So off they went to the parrot and the little creature said,
'Excuse me please, but can you tell me who I am?'

'You have a wonderful long snout,' squawked the parrot, 'but I don't know who you are. Let us go to the anthill and ask the anteater.'

So off they all went to the anteater and the little creature said, 'Excuse me please, but do you know who I am?'

The anteater took its snout out of the anthill and said, 'Well, you have the most amazing twitching whiskers, but I don't know who you are. Let us go to the wheat field and ask the harvest mouse.'

So off they all went to the harvest mouse and the little creature said, 'Excuse me, have you any idea who I am?'

'You have a tongue that flickers and is as quick as lightning,' whispered the harvest mouse, 'but I don't know who you are. Let us go to the desert and ask the snake.'

So off they all went to the snake and the little creature said,
'Can you help me? I've no idea who I am.'

The snake slithered up close for a good look and said, 'You have a mane the colour of gold, but I don't know who you are. Let us go to the savannah and ask the lion.'

So off they all went to the
lion and the little creature said,
'Excuse me please, can you help?
I'm trying to find out who I am.'

The lion yawned and said, 'You have wings that glitter like cathedral windows. I have never seen such wonderful wings, but even I don't know who you are. Let us go to the pond and ask the dragonfly.'

So off they all went to the dragonfly and when the dragonfly had stopped flitting about the little creature said, 'Excuse me please, but I'm longing to know who I am. Can you help me?'

'Your fur is as red as the sunset,' sang the dragonfly,
'but I don't know who you are. Let us go and ask the fox.'

By now all the animals were getting a little tired, but nevertheless, they went to the fox and the little creature said, 'Excuse me please, I'd love to know who I am. Can you help me?'

'You have a tail that is as black as night,' said the fox, 'but even with all my cunning I couldn't begin to guess who you are. Let us go and ask the cat.'

So off they all went to the cat and the little creature said, 'Excuse me please, but nobody seems to know who I am. Can you help me?'

'What is the first thing you discovered about yourself?' asked the cat.

'I saw my reflection in a frozen pond,' said the little creature, 'and my eyes were as big and bright as the moon.'

'Then you must go and ask the owl,' said the cat.

And so they all went to the owl and the little creature said,
'Excuse me please, but can you tell me who I am?'

And the wise old owl said, 'Why, of course I can. You are a bit of everything ... the rarest, most wonderful creature of all. You are ...

... Little Hotchpotch!'